My Truck Is Stuck!

MY TRUCK

Kevin Lewis and Daniel Kirk

SCHOLASTIC INC.
New York Toronto London Auckland Sydney
Mexico City New Delhi Hong Kong Buenos Aires

ISBN-13: 978-0-545-13904-5
ISBN-10: 0-545-13904-X

Text copyright © 2002 by Kevin Lewis.
Illustrations copyright © 2002 by Daniel Kirk.
All rights reserved. Published by Scholastic Inc.,
557 Broadway, New York, NY 10012, by arrangement
with Hyperion Books for Children, an imprint of
Disney Children's Book Group, LLC. SCHOLASTIC and
associated logos are trademarks and/or registered
trademarks of Scholastic Inc.

12 11 10 9 8 7 6   9 10 11 12 13/0

Printed in the U.S.A.   08

First Scholastic printing, November 2008

The artwork for this book was prepared using oil paint
over sand and modeling paste on masonite.

For my brother David
—K.L.

For Russell's teachers
Deb Cook
Lisa Walter
Diana Bendin
Jerry Juzdan
Cindy Barrow
—D.K.

Dump truck comin'
down the road.
Dump truck haulin'
a great big load.
Round and round,
the wheels they roll.
Round and round . . .

into a hole!

"Rotten luck. Can't go!
My truck is stuck."

Gears grind.
The engine roars.
But the truck won't go.

Not one inch more.

"Help!
Please help!

Does anyone know
how to make
my stuck truck go?"

HELP! PLEASE HELP!

BOW-WOW

beep!
beep!

Here comes a car.
Full of travelers,
traveling far.

"Rotten luck. Can't go. My truck is stuck."

Tug and tow. **2** engines roar.
But the truck won't go. Not one inch more.

"**Help!
Please help!**
Does anyone know
how to make
my stuck truck go?"

beep!
beep!

**Here comes a van,
driven by
a moving man.**

"Rotten luck. Can't go. My truck is stuck."

Drag and draw. Tug and tow.
3 engines roar.
But the truck won't go.

"Help!
Please help!
Does anyone know
how to make
my stuck truck go?"

beep!
beep!

Here comes a Jeep,
up a hillside
very steep.

"Rotten luck. Can't go. My truck is stuck!"

Heft and haul. Tug and tow.
4 engines roar.
The truck still won't go.

"Help!
Please help!
Does anyone know
how to make
my stuck truck go?"

beep!
beep!

Here comes a bus
full of youngsters.
What a fuss!

"Rotten luck. Can't go. My truck is stuck!"

Lug and lurch. Tug and tow.
5 engines roar.
The truck won't go. . . .

GO TEAM GO!

honk! honk!

No need to panic!
Here comes a tow truck
with a mechanic.

"Mr. Mechanic,
I'm sure you know
how to make
my stuck truck go!"

"Sure! To move it
on its way,
just hook it up
and then you'll say—

"What luck! My truck's not stuck!"

vroom!
vroom!

Now car and van
and Jeep and bus
all move on
without a fuss.

And the dump truck rolls
on down the road
on its way to deliver

a great big load.